Akua

Chase and the Case of the Missing Jersey

Written by: Cousin John

Illustrated by: Catienna Regis

The world is yours!

This book is dedicated to Chase and Jaxson.

Chase began his day feeling nervous and blue.

He couldn't find his favorite jersey, and he didn't know what to do.

Chase looked everywhere, turning his room upside down.

He was so angry and couldn't help but frown.

"Have you seen my jersey?"

Chase asked his mom.

She said no, but told Chase that

he should stay calm.

"Where was the last place you saw it?"

His mom asked.

Chase had no idea. So his mom gave

him a new task.

"I know you're upset," she said.

"But take a deep breath."

"Instead of getting angry, try retracing your steps."

Chase took a deep breath, and it put

his mind at ease.

He suddenly realized where his jersey might be.

Chase quickly put on his shoes

and rushed out the door.

He ran so fast, that his feet barely touched the floor.

Chase arrived at his Uncle Devon's house after

retracing his steps.

"Is my favorite jersey here?" Chase asked while

trying to catch his breath.

"Sorry," said Uncle Devon. "It's not here."

Chase began to worry that his favorite jersey may have disappeared.

"What did the jersey look like?" asked Uncle Devon.

Chase told him it was blue and had his favorite number, eleven.

Uncle Devon's eyes lit up, and his fingers snapped.

"I saw your friend Gavin

wearing a jersey just like that."

Chase couldn't believe that Gavin would steal his

favorite jersey.

He was angry and marched to Gavin's house

in a hurry.

"Give me back my jersey," said Chase.

"This isn't fair!"

But Gavin just stood there with a blank stare.

"We don't wear the same size," said Gavin.

"Your jersey would never fit."

"Besides, my jersey has my name on the back of it."

Chase was embarrassed that he thought his friend was stealing.

"I'm sorry," said Chase.

"I didn't mean to hurt your feelings."

Chase was still worried about his jersey. He asked for help after apologizing to his friend.

"Of course," said Gavin. "But first, you need to calm down by counting backwards from ten."

Ten…nine…eight

Chase was beginning to feel a little better.

Seven..six…five..four

He began to relax a little bit more.

Chase counted from three, all the way down to one

When he reached zero, all of the anger

that he felt was done.

Now it was time to get back to the task at hand.

Where was Chase's jersey?

He just couldn't understand.

Chase decided to go home again
and check on a shelf.

He even called more friends for some extra help.

The friends searched everywhere. They looked high and low.

Each friend had something about the jersey that they wanted to know.

"When was the last time you wore it?" asked Mike

Tina asked if Chase wore it last week to ride his bike.

All of these questions were
spinning in Chase's head.

That's when his friends noticed that
he was turning red.

Chase tried to take a deep breath, but that
was no fix.

He started to count backwards from ten, but
quit before he got to six.

The anger was building up, and Chase wanted to cry.

That's when Emy said Chase should give something new a try.

Emy explained, "We all have days where something goes wrong."

"It helps me clear my head when I sing a song."

Chase decided to give it a try.

Suddenly, while he was singing, a thought came to mind.

Chase loved his favorite jersey so much

that he always liked to keep it clean.

He forgot that he asked his mom to put

it in the washing machine.

Chase ran to the washing machine

and guess what he found?

His favorite jersey was there waiting for him.

It was safe and sound.

Chase was happy he found his jersey.

But he found something else that he liked best.

Thanks to his friends, Chase had some new

ways to deal with stress.

About the Author

John Butler, known as Cousin John, is a Philadelphia native, educator and sports journalist who has turned his passion for writing into a series of children's books. To discover additional stories in this series, visit ChaseBooks.com.

Made in the USA
Middletown, DE
05 November 2022

13929592R00024